For all my family ~ M.H.

For Dee ~ C.W.

First published in the United States 1996 by
Little Tiger Press,
12221 West Feerick Street, Wauwatosa, WI 53222-2117

Originally published in Great Britain 1995 by
Magi Publications, London

Text © 1995 Martin Hall
Illustrations © 1995 Catherine Walters

CIP Data is available.

Printed in Belgium

First American Edition

ISBN 1-888444-06-1

1 3 5 7 9 10 8 6 4 2

January '97
For Tristan,
On the occasion of
your 6th birthday!
A special that made us
think of your dog "Checkers".
Enjoy — god bless you!
Love,
the Glasgows

Charlie and Tess

by Martin Hall

Pictures by Catherine Walters

Little Tiger Press

It was spring, and lambing time high up in the mountains. But the weather was still cold, and snow was falling, so the farmer was out tending the flock with his sheepdog. The farmer stopped and listened. What was that noise? It sounded like a frightened bleating. Ahead he saw a tiny lamb, alone and hungry.

"My, you're a small one," the farmer said. "Can't find your mother, eh? Well, you'll just have to come home with me."

In the kitchen the farmer's daughter, Emily, made the lamb a cozy nest in a cardboard box with some old sweaters. He was very weak, but was soon sucking warm milk from a bottle. "Let's call him Charlie," said Emily. And because they could find no ewe to take care of him, Charlie became the family's own special pet and lived with them in the farmhouse.

The farmer's sheepdog was named Tess, and as soon as
Charlie was able to skip and frisk around the farmyard,
Tess was there to keep an eye on him. She made sure he
did not stray too far and led him home at feeding time.
And when Charlie was too old for the milk bottle,
Tess showed him the best pastures to graze in.

Charlie grew quickly. Soon he was too big for the box in the kitchen, so he slept outside in Tess' doghouse. It was a tight squeeze, but Tess and Charlie didn't mind. For they were friends, and kept each other warm.

They played together when Tess was not working.
The farmer would throw a ball and watch them both
chase it. Of course, Tess was faster than Charlie, but often
she would let the lamb win.
"Sometimes I wonder if Charlie is turning into a dog,"
Emily's mother said one day as the family watched him play.

Charlie even had his own collar
and leash. When Emily's mother
went into town, Tess and Charlie
would go along, too. People would
laugh and point as Charlie trotted
ahead, often carrying a newspaper
in his mouth.

All too soon Charlie grew too big for the doghouse. It was time for him to join the rest of the flock.

Charlie missed his adopted family up on the mountainside, and Tess was lonely without her friend, and whined every night by her doghouse.

"Never mind, old girl," soothed the farmer. "We'll see Charlie soon enough when we move the flock to the next pasture."

But that was when the trouble started. As soon as the farmer and Tess began to herd the sheep to a new field, Charlie wanted to round up the flock, too.

"Charlie! Go back with the other sheep," laughed the farmer. But Charlie was determined to help Tess, and the farmer had to push him back into the flock again.

This went on all summer, because Charlie thought he was a sheepdog.

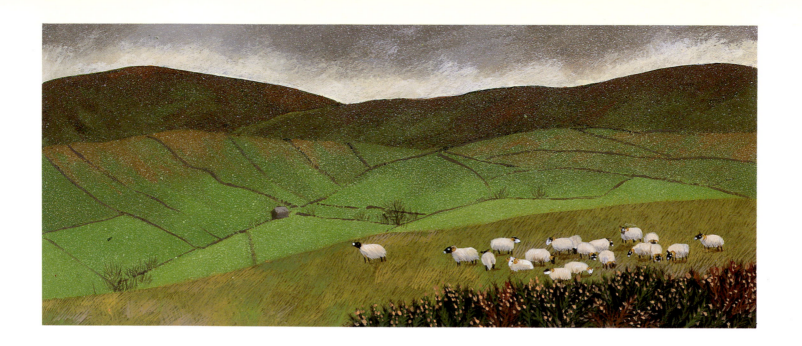

Summer turned to autumn, and then it was nearly
winter again. One day the sky was filled with clouds
the color of slate. Charlie sniffed the air. It reminded
him of a time long ago, when he was lost and alone.
It grew colder and colder, and the wind began to blow.
The sheep huddled together, but there was little shelter.
Then it began to snow.

Charlie baaed anxiously.
Snowflakes began to settle on his fleece.
Where was Tess? Where was the farmer?
If they didn't come soon, snow would bury
the whole flock.

The snow piled up quickly, and some of the
weaker sheep could barely walk through the drifts.
If they didn't move into the valley quickly it would
be too late.

Charlie knew just what to do. He ran ahead of the flock, baaing loudly. He turned back and butted the other sheep, pulling at their woolly coats with his teeth. He raced backward and forward, until finally the flock began to move down the mountainside toward shelter.

The next day the storm died down, and a low sun shone orange across the snow-covered hills. The farmer was at last able to go out and search for his flock.

"I'm really worried – I don't know if we will be able to find them," he said to Tess, looking at the mountains. "The snow must be even deeper up there."

Tess ran ahead, and the farmer began to struggle up the mountainside. Suddenly the sheepdog bounded toward the farmer and started barking and tugging at his trousers.

"What have you found, girl?" he asked.

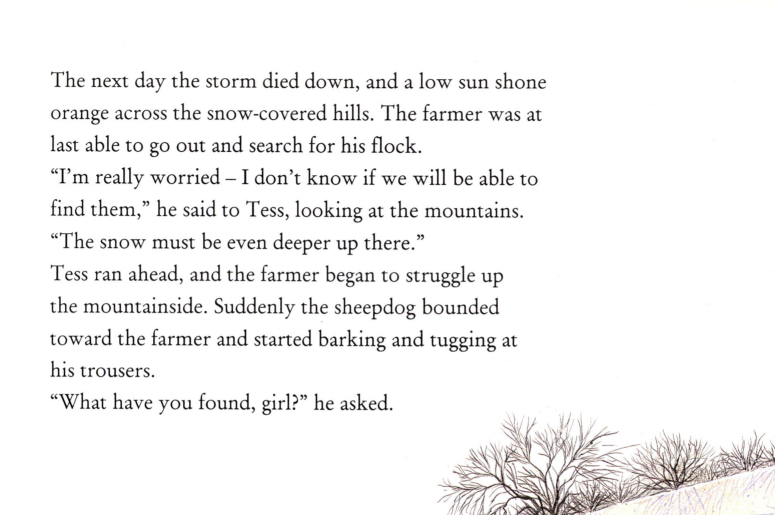

Tess led the farmer back into the valley along a narrow trail.
At the end of the path the farmer stopped, amazed. His whole
flock was safely gathered there in a sheltered hollow.
"Charlie! This must have been you," the farmer said.
"You saved the whole flock from the snowstorm.
You really are a sheepdog after all!"
"Woof!" Tess agreed.
"Baa," said Charlie proudly.